Foods for the Future

Saskia Lacey

Publishing Credits
Corinne Burton, M.A.Ed., *President*
Conni Medina, M.A.Ed., *Managing Editor*
Diana Kenney, M.A.Ed., NBCT, *Content Director*
Emily R. Smith, M.A.Ed., *Series Developer*
Courtney Patterson, *Multimedia Designer*

Image Credits: Cover, 2–3, 7–32: Travis Hanson; all other images: Shutterstock

Library of Congress Cataloging-in-Publication Data

Lacey, Saskia, author.
 Foods for the future / Saskia Lacey.
    pages cm
 Summary: "The year is 2052. A group of young chefs is hoping to make new breakthroughs in the world of sustainable foods. They are a part of an international online cooking community called The Flavorium. Each dish they make uses eco-friendly (and sometimes gross!) ingredients. The results aren't always pretty, but The Flavorium is determined to create a sustainable future. They will do anything-and eat anything-to solve global environmental issues."-- Provided by publisher.
  Audience: Grades 4 to 6.
  ISBN 978-1-4938-1295-0 (pbk.)
 1. Food--Juvenile literature. 2. Food supply--Juvenile literature. 3. Sustainable living--Juvenile literature. I. Title.
 TX355.L134 2016
 641.3--dc23
                                              2015015657

Teacher Created Materials

5301 Oceanus Drive
Huntington Beach, CA 92649-1030
http://www.tcmpub.com
ISBN 978-1-4938-1295-0
© 2016 Teacher Created Materials, Inc.
Made in China
Nordica.082015.CA21501053

FLAVORIUM
Foods for the Future

Story Summary

The year is 2052. A group of young chefs hopes to make new breakthroughs in the world of sustainable foods. They are a part of an international online cooking community called *The Flavorium*. Each dish they make uses eco-friendly (and sometimes gross!) ingredients. The results aren't always pretty, but The Flavorium is determined to create a sustainable future. They will do anything—and eat anything—to solve global environmental issues.

In this book, matters of food sustainability are based in science but may leave room for interpretation. Remember, this story is a work of fiction and character opinions are provided solely for the purpose of telling a fictional story.

Tips for Performing Reader's Theater

Adapted from Aaron Shepard

★ Don't let your script hide your face. If you can't see the audience, your script is too high.

★ Look up often when you speak. Don't just look at your script.

★ Talk slowly so the audience knows what you are saying.

★ Talk loudly so everyone can hear you.

★ Talk with feeling. If the character is sad, let your voice be sad. If the character is surprised, let your voice be surprised.

★ Stand up straight. Keep your hands and feet still.

★ Remember that even when you are not talking, you are still your character.

★ If the audience laughs, wait for them to stop before you speak again.

★ If someone in the audience talks, don't pay attention.

★ If someone walks into the room, don't pay attention.

★ If you make a mistake, pretend it was right.

★ If you drop something, try to leave it where it is until the audience is looking somewhere else.

★ If a reader forgets to read his or her part, see if you can read the part instead, make something up, or just skip over it. Don't whisper to the reader!

Foods for the Future

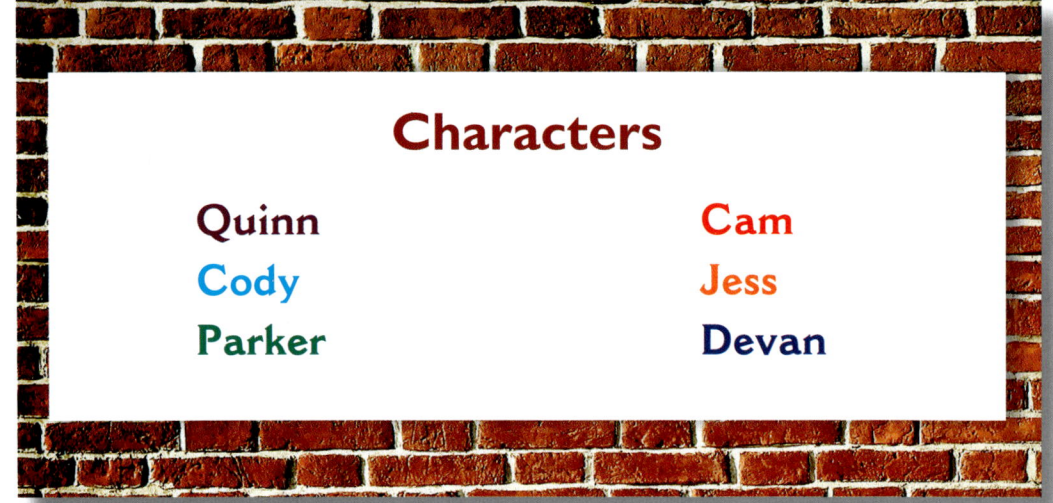

Characters

Quinn   Cam
Cody   Jess
Parker   Devan

Setting

This story takes place in the year 2052, deep in the foodie blogosphere, on a website called *The Flavorium*. The website is devoted to creating eco-friendly dishes.

Act I

Quinn: I'm super excited to begin this week's webisode!

Cody: Me, too. I think our eco-foodies are really going to appreciate these extraordinary dishes.

Quinn: When we created this blog a few years ago, I never dreamed we'd have so many followers. Who knew there were this many people interested in global food security?

Cody: Right? I mean, I didn't even know what global food security meant until you explained it to me.

Quinn: Don't knock yourself too hard. It's one of those important issues that doesn't get the airtime it deserves. I think people are just starting to realize that our current farming system isn't working. The truth is, it hasn't been working for a long, long time.

Cody: Yep, the way we produce food has to change, or it will be impossible to create a sustainable future.

Quinn: Agreed. Otherwise, things could get really bad. There may come a day when we will not have the food or energy to sustain our global population. And then, it's goodbye, food security; hello, world famine.

Cody: Sometimes I feel like we should be doing even more to help the environment. I want to believe that the website is enough, but then I worry that The Flavorium only appeals to people who are already eco-minded. Do you think our website is actually making a difference?

Quinn: I really do. We are gaining new viewers every day. As long as we continue to make webisodes that teach people about how they can protect our environment, we are doing our part.

Cody: Oh my gosh! Is it two o'clock already? We have to go live in 15 minutes.

Quinn: We should check in with The Flavorium and make sure the chefs are ready to begin the show.

Cody: Let's start with Parker in San Francisco. Park is making the appetizers and will be streaming first.

Quinn: Parker's up on video chat. Good.

Cody: Are you ready, Park? We'll be going live in a few minutes.

Parker: I am, and you guys are going to *love* this dish. Hint: you can hear these whenever Cody tells a joke.

Quinn: Crickets?

Cody: From London, we'll head to New York City's favorite borough, Brooklyn! There, Devan will serve us today's main course. I might be incorrect, but I heard that Devan will be cooking with a 3-D food printer.

Quinn: Can't wait for that one.

Cody: All right, let's kick things off. Parker, how's the weather on the West Coast?

Parker: Foggy as usual. It feels like the whole city is sitting on a cloud. I love it!

Cody: To each his or her own. I prefer shorts weather. The hotter the better, I say!

Quinn: Guys, let's get back on topic. The show is only a half hour.

Parker: Yikes, I always forget that the show is so short! Okay, today I will be making my Country Cricket Cookies. They're not exactly appetizers, but I couldn't resist bringing them on today's show.

Cody: Did you say crickets?

Parker: I did. As you know, the United Nations has been making the case for edible insects for some time.

Quinn: Why are insects a viable, sustainable food?

Parker: Well, they are a fantastic source of protein and they produce very few greenhouse gases. In comparison to other protein sources, such as cows and chickens, they require very little water, food, and energy. If you're trying to make eco-friendly, nutritious meals, you can't do much better than crickets. I could go on!

Quinn: Please do. Could you explain in greater detail how eating insects benefits global food security? Actually, why don't you begin by describing the current state of food production? Cody and I were talking off air, and we realized that many people still don't know what the phrase "global food security" actually means.

Parker: That is a great question. Basically, having global food security means we have the ability to produce enough food to feed everyone on Earth for the foreseeable future. In the last 50 years, the world population has grown by two billion, which means there are nearly nine billion people living on Earth today! As the United Nations predicted, we have had to increase our food production by 60 percent to feed our global community.

Cody: Which hasn't been easy.

Parker: No, not at all. Food costs have risen substantially and, as you know, meat has become especially expensive. Soon, turkey and beef will be viewed as delicacies.

Act 2

Quinn: Welcome to another webisode with The Flavorium. We're reporting live from the heart of The Flavorium community: Cody's kitchen!

Cody: And it's actually clean.

Quinn: Honestly, I almost didn't recognize it.

Cody: Quinn and I are super excited about this latest webisode we've cooked up for you because we have four fantastic Flavorium chefs making appearances today.

Quinn: Remember to send us your questions and comments throughout the show. We will select a few foodie messages to respond to at the end of the webisode.

Cody: Let's get started. In today's show, we will be cooking a hi-tech, three-course, eco-friendly meal.

Quinn: That's three courses of delicious, sustainable goodness!

Cody: We will begin with Parker, our appetizer chef, in San Francisco.

Quinn: Then, we'll travel across the pond to talk with Cam and Jess in London. They will be cooking the first course.

Parker: You got it, Quinn!

Cody: You guys are terrible! I'm checking in with Cameron and Jess.

Jess: Hey, Cody. We're all set. Do you still want Cam and me to host the second part of the show?

Cody: If you could, that would be fantastic. We want to switch things up a bit, and you'll be hosting Devan's segment.

Jess: Awesome! We're huge fans of Devan.

Cody: Speaking of which…is Devan online yet?

Devan: I'm here, and I'm ready!

Quinn: Okay, it looks like we're good to go.

Cody: Quinn, we've already got around 100,000 foodies logged in.

Quinn: That's a record. I told you The Flavorium is making a difference. There is hope! Cody, my esteemed co-host, are you ready to go live?

Cody: Ready!

Poem: "Hope" is the thing with feathers

Quinn: The livestock industry has been such a huge source of energy consumption.

Parker: It takes ridiculous quantities of water and food to maintain livestock.

Cody: Did you guys know that 36 percent of food from our crops goes to feeding livestock? Like, how is that even possible? Our major sources of food are being wasted on each other.

Parker: And it's all to support the world's unhealthy appetite for animal products! Our bodies don't require anywhere near as much meat as we currently consume, and don't even get me started on the connection between greenhouse gas emissions and livestock!

Quinn: The livestock industry is the primary source of greenhouse gas emissions, correct?

Parker: Absolutely; agriculture emits far more greenhouse gases than our transportation does, including cars, trains, and planes combined.

Cody: Wow. That, I didn't know.

Parker: Let's get back to the crickets. I don't want to take up too much time on the show.

Quinn: Don't worry. This is important.

Cody: Obvious question: do crickets actually taste good?

Parker: It depends on how you prepare them. For the novice insect eater, I think it's best to start with cricket flour.

Cody: How do you make cricket flour?

Parker: First, I purchase crickets from an insect farm, or in other words, a farm that raises insects made to be consumed by humans. In order to make cricket flour, I dry-roast the crickets and then mill them into powder. I combine this powder with almond meal to create the flour, and then I use the cricket flour as I would any other flour.

Quinn: That's amazing. I can't wait to try these cookies.

Cody: Is it wrong that I feel bad for the crickets?

Quinn: You're such a softie.

Cody: If it were possible, I wouldn't eat any living thing—but unfortunately, that's not a practical diet. Park, we want our viewers to be able to make these cookies, so can you post the full recipe on the website?

Parker: Sure. By the way, I got this recipe from Hop Hop, a fantastic San Francisco bakery that utilizes only cricket flour.

Cody: Hop Hop. Clever.

Quinn: Great name!

Parker: I've just posted the recipe on The Flavorium for anyone who would like to make Country Cricket Cookies.

Quinn: Parker was kind enough to send Cody and me a batch of cookies. Are you ready to try them, Cody?

Cody: As ready as I'll ever be.

Parker: Let's all eat them together!

Cody: On the count of three: one, two,—

Quinn: Bite!

Parker: Delicious! What do you guys think?

Quinn: These taste quite good.

Cody: I'm surprised. Park, you may have actually converted me to insect eating.

Quinn: Is there a word for an insect eater, like *insectarian* instead of *vegetarian*?

Parker: Close. *Entomophagy* is the practice of eating insects.

Cody: That wasn't close to *insectarian* at all!

Quinn: Thanks for the recipe, Park. Foodies, if you have any questions for Parker, write to us and we'll try to answer them at the end of the program.

Cody: Park, stick around for the rest of the show because it's definitely going to be a good one.

Parker: Thanks guys, and I had fun as always. I'd love to stay on for the rest of the show.

Cody: Ok, now we'll be handing over the reins of the last courses to two of your favorite chefs, Cam and Jess. Quinn and I will see you again at the end of the show.

Cam: Hi, everybody! Jess and I are thrilled to host the last two courses.

Jess: We've been a part of The Flavorium for a long time and are so thankful to Quinn and Cory for giving us a chance to discuss the global issues that we feel most passionate about.

Cam: Ok, let's get started.

Jess: Wait, Parker—are you still with us?

Parker: I am!

Cam: Oops, didn't mean to forget you, Parker. Thank you for making us a batch of your awesome cricket cookies. We were really nervous about the idea of eating creepy crawly insects, but now we can't stop eating them.

Parker: I'm so glad that you're enjoying them.

Cam: Jess has already eaten four cookies today. Hey Jess, stop eating the cookies; you need to stay hungry for the next two courses.

Jess: I can't help it! OK. I'll stop.

Cam: Eco-foodies, we have something very special to share with you today.

Jess: Yep! Today is the day we are introducing our latest culinary invention.

Cam: For the last two years—that's *seven hundred and thirty days*—Jess and I have been hard at work pondering a solution to our current sustainability issues.

Jess: After many failed attempts, we finally think that we might have something that will greatly improve our global food security. We would like to introduce Soytein, our eco-superfood!

Parker: What exactly is Soytein? It's a shake, right? A nutritious shake?

Cam: It's more than that, because Soytein contains every essential vitamin and nutrient a person needs to maintain a healthy diet.

Parker: Whoa, this is some seriously futuristic stuff.

Jess: If necessary, you could drink Soytein for every meal and be perfectly healthy.

Parker: Cool! How is drinking Soytein beneficial for our environment?

Jess: Well, for starters, it doesn't take much energy to produce Soytein. We don't need many of the crops, animals, or other things normally involved in food production. All of our packaging is recyclable, and portion size is carefully measured so that people only eat what they need and do not waste food.

Parker: That makes sense, and it comes in powder form, correct?

Cam: Yes, which also means less waste, which is a big plus for our environment.

Jess: This might be a good time to segue into food waste and how it impacts our environment. We were going to wait until later in the program, but this seems like a good opportunity. Cam, why is the reduction of food waste so important?

Cam: Most people don't think much about food waste. They worry about plastic and other non-biodegradable items, but throwing away food isn't good for our environment either. We throw away millions of tons of quality food every year, and the majority of it ends up buried in landfills.

Parker: Whoa, I didn't know that.

Jess: Yeah, it's a huge problem. Food might be biodegradable, but it still releases methane into the air. Methane is one of the most harmful greenhouse gases.

Parker: Food releases methane? That's crazy.

Jess: Yes, and that's why it's so important not to waste food, even if people decide not to buy a product like Soytein.

Parker: What exactly is in the powder?

Jess: We can't give you the exact recipe, as we are hoping to sell Soytein to consumers in the future. But we've included a free sample link on our website for all Flavorium viewers.

Parker: That's awesome! Eco-foodies, be sure to take advantage of Cam and Jess's free Soytein sample.

Cam: Are you ready to take your first sip, Parker?

Parker: More than ready. Hmm. It tastes kind of…chalky?

Cam: I've heard that before!

Parker: It also tastes a bit like strawberries…strawberries mixed with tree bark.

Cam: That, I've never heard.

Jess: Park, how do you even know what bark tastes like?

Parker: I'm an adventurous foodie, Jess.

Jess: I guess so!

Cam: So, what do you think?

Parker: I'm not completely sold on the taste, but I do like the idea of a meal that has such a small ecological footprint.

Cam: The taste does need some improvement, so we're still trying to come up with a recipe that is as palatable as it is nutritious.

Parker: I'm sure you guys will! Is there anything else you would like to say about Soytein?

Jess: Yes, one last thing. In the future, we hope Soytein will help feed the world's hungry. We believe our product is perfect for mass distribution in countries that are dealing with famine.

Parker: That's wonderful. I can see that you both have grand ambitions for this product.

Cam: That's an understatement—but we've just got to make it taste good first!

Jess: We would love it if Soytein were successful. Mostly because it would mean that we were making great strides towards global food security. However, we would be equally as happy if people made a commitment to reduce their food waste. It's time to make big changes in our daily lives.

Parker: I completely agree, and please keep The Flavorium updated about your Soytein experiments!

Cam: We definitely will.

Parker: All right, guys, I'm signing off for now. Enjoy your talk with Devan!

Jess: Thanks, Parker, see you in a bit.

Act 4

Cam: For those eco-foodies who are just joining us, The Flavorium has cooked up a great show for you. We are making a three course eco-friendly meal, and we've already spoken with Parker about cricket cookies.

Jess: Delicious cricket cookies!

Cam: Yes, surprisingly delicious.

Jess: And Cam and I have just finished talking about our newest product, Soytein.

Cam: Now, we will be tuning in with Devan in Brooklyn. Devan will be cooking a meal using a 3-D food printer.

Devan: Hi there. It's actually called the *Cyburg*. This 3-D food printer specializes in hamburgers. It has taken decades to perfect, but we have finally been able to create a totally edible lab-made burger.

Cam: How exactly does one make a burger in a lab? How can you make beef without a cow?

Jess: Yeah, that kind of seems impossible!

Devan: It's very difficult, but it is possible. We took the cells from a cow's shoulder muscle, and using a special solution, we were able to multiply the cells. Then, the cells developed into muscle cells. Finally, the muscle cells became strips of muscle fiber.

Jess: Are you saying that you've literally been growing meat? What a weird concept.

Devan: Yep.

Cam: Wow, if we can grow meat in a lab, we can eliminate the need for a huge part of the livestock industry. The positive impact of such a scientific breakthrough cannot be overstated.

Devan: I agree. As our world population grows, more and more communities are demanding a meat-based diet. This demand has already created a lot of problems for our environment. As you said earlier, the livestock industry is draining our food, water, and energy resources. The Cyburg offers a possible solution to these problems.

Cam: So cool.

Devan: I know, we are very excited! Another benefit of growing meat in a lab is that it will free up an enormous amount of agricultural space for different crops.

Jess: Which is so needed.

Devan: Yes, we really need to diversify our crops if we want to maintain global food security.

Cam: What do you mean when you say "diversify our crops"?

Devan: Well, for example, most of our agricultural space is being taken up by only a few types of crops, such as wheat and rice. If those crops were hit by disease or drought, the results would be devastating. We need to diversify our crops so that we are not dependent on any one crop for our survival. That way, if something goes wrong, we'll still have plenty to eat.

Jess: That's so interesting. Devan, did you want to show us how the Cyburg works?

Devan: I'd love to! The Cyburg is a lot like other 3-D printers, except our end product will be a tasty hamburger. First, I will input the ingredient capsules into the printer. Then, I will type in the meal that we would like the printer to prepare. Finally, the machine will begin printing out the burger, layer by layer.

Jess: How long does it take to make one burger, cooked and all?

Devan: It takes about 30 seconds. We're trying to cut that time down to 10–15 seconds. We know how impatient people are today.

Cam: I don't know, 30 seconds sounds pretty fast to me!

Jess: Me, too!

Devan: Our first burger should be done by now. Time for a taste test!

Cam: I can't believe I'm going to eat an actual Cyburg! Do you remember when scientists first started working on lab burgers? It cost thousands of dollars just to create *one* burger.

Jess: I barely remember. It seems like so long ago.

Cam: Devan, thanks for sending over the 3-D Cyburg printers. We will put them to good use. Now, let's eat some lab-made burgers.

Jess: Oh, wow. This is delicious. I think I might even like this dish more than Parker's fantastic cricket cookies.

Parker: Hey, not cool!

Cam: Parker! We thought you were offline. I feel guilty agreeing with Jess, but this Cyburg is super tasty! That doesn't mean the cricket cookies weren't delicious.

Parker: I'm going to have to eat one to believe it. Devan, can you send me a Cyburg printer, too?

Devan: Only if you send me a batch of Country Cricket Cookies.

Parker: Done!

Jess: Devan, these Cyburgs taste exactly like the real thing. I might switch over to eating only meat that is produced from animal cells.

Cam: Who thought you'd ever be able to say such a thing?

Jess: Not me!

Devan: Hey, didn't Cody and Quinn say they were going to answer questions at the end of the program?

Jess: Oh, my gosh! Is it two-thirty already?

Devan: Almost; we only have about five minutes left. Cody and Quinn, want to close out the show?

Quinn: And, we're back! Devan, thanks for reminding us. All right eco-foodies, we're going to spend the last few minutes of the show reading some of your questions and comments.

Cody: Let's see. Here's a good one: Jenna from Seattle just wrote in with a recipe for cicada (si-KEY-duh) cookies. Parker, this is right up your alley.

Parker: Send that recipe to me! I've never tried cicada cookies.

Cody: Thanks, Jenna; we'll definitely try out the cicada cookies. If they're a hit with The Flavorium, we may invite you to do a segment on the show.

Quinn: This next one is a question from Adam from Chicago. Adam wants to know how he can buy a Cyburg printer. Devan, are you still with us?

Devan: I'm still here! Our Cyburgs are not yet available for purchase. We're still fine-tuning a few things. We want to develop the patties in a variety of beef flavors. Some of the patties will taste as if they are cooked well-done. Other patties will taste as if they have been cooked medium-rare. We want this product to be enjoyed by as many people as possible. It's important that the first experience the public has with this product is positive.

Quinn: I'm so glad you are taking your time developing this product. There is a lot riding on the success of the Cyburg. As you said, we really want the public to have a positive experience. Unfortunately, in this case, positive means *tasty* and not *eco-friendly*. Despite all the issues we are currently facing, consumers still value pleasure over practicality.

Devan: Yes, the bottom line is that it doesn't matter how eco-friendly a product is, because if they don't like it, they won't buy it. So, we're taking our time. Long story short: we're hoping to have Cyburgs on the market in about six months. We will let you know when they will be available for preorder.

Cody: Thanks, Devan. Okay, we're just about out of time. Quinn, let's quickly review the five big ideas of the day.

Quinn: Okay, I'll start. Big idea one: Insects are a healthy, eco-friendly protein alternative.

Parker: Yeah!

Cody: Big idea two: We need to eat fewer animal products. The livestock industry is threatening our global food security.

Devan: Unless, the animal products are grown in a lab.

Cody: Of course.

Quinn: Big idea three: Food waste, even though biodegradable, is harmful to the planet. Therefore, only buy and prepare what you can eat.

Cody: Big idea four: Lab-made burgers are tasty?

Jess: Yes, yes, they are.

Devan: Thanks, guys!

Cody: Big idea five: Crop diversity is important. We need to grow many different types of crops so that we are not dependent on any one crop for food.

Quinn: That's right. And that's all for today's webisode. We hope you'll take what you've learned today and help us make a better, brighter future! See you next week, same time, same place. Bye, eco-foodies!

🎵 Song: Sweet By and By 🎵

"Hope" is the thing with feathers

by Emily Dickenson

"Hope" is the thing with feathers
That perches in the soul,
And sings the tune without the words,
And never stops at all,

And sweetest in the gale is heard;
And sore must be the storm
That could abash the little bird
That kept so many warm.

I've heard it in chillest land,
And on the strangest sea;
Yet, never, in extremity,
It asked a crumb of me.

Sweet By and By
by Sanford F. Bennett

In the sweet by and by,
We shall meet on that shore;
In the sweet by and by,
We shall meet on that beautiful shore.
We shall sing on that beautiful shore
The melodious songs of the blessed;
And our spirits shall sorrow no more,
Not a sigh for the blessing of rest.

This is an abridged version of the original song.

Glossary

agriculture—the practice of growing crops and raising livestock

diversify—to change something so that it has more kinds of people or things

eco-friendly—not harmful to the environment

emissions—things produced or sent out, such as energy or gas from a source

entomophagy—the practice of eating insects

famine—a situation in which many people do not have enough food to eat

foodies—people who enjoy and care about food

non-biodegradable—incapable of being slowly destroyed and broken down into very small parts by natural processes, bacteria, etc.

production—the process of making or growing something for sale or use

sustainable—able to be used without being completely used up or destroyed